14 DAYS — NOT RENEWABLE *thrice*

Please Don't Lose the Date Card

"OLD CHAIRS TO MEND."

ISRAEL R. POTTER

Born in Cranston R.I. August 1st 1744.

The Testament ❋ of Israel Potter

❋ by WILLIAM DORESKI

SEVEN WOODS PRESS
NEW YORK
1976

Seven Woods Press books are published by George Koppelman. For information direct inquiries to:

Seven Woods Press
Post Office Box 32, Village Station
New York, New York 10014

Publication of this book is supported by a grant from the National Endowment for the Arts in Washington, D.C., a Federal agency.

Library of Congress Cataloging in Publication Data
Doreski, William
The testament of Israel Potter.

Includes bibliographical references.
1. Potter, Israel Ralph, 1744-1826?--Poetry.
I. Title.
PS3554.O67T4   811'.5'4   76-8902
ISBN 0-913282-06-5
ISBN 0-913282-07-3 pbk.
ISBN 0-913282-08-1 signed ltd.

For MY MOTHER
and FATHER

LIST OF ILLUSTRATIONS

THE TESTAMENT OF ISRAEL POTTER

Dear wife: the sea-wind mimics
the veteran's fading croak. These states
I thought had swept out the Tories,
but from my hotel window I
watch Boston Harbor merchantmen
disgorge marked crates of export-ware
and tea from English wholesalers.

You failed to live to see me home:
on these shores I'm just a relic,
some curio beached after years.
Surprised? Not so surprised as I
to find I can talk shamelessly
hour on hour to the dead.
Forgive me: I outlived you
only to play you for a saint;
forgive me that I make you listen.

Let me ramble---- you've heard so much,
how I dropped root in England,
then later and willing in you.
I was born in the Colonies:
in Cranston, where slimy fishboats
and schooners tack Narragansett
Bay to dock in Providence,
our only city named for God.

Even now, aged seventy-nine
and lisping for lack of teeth,
I can claim a few decent years
when a boy near the ocean
where the rain fell tasty with salt.
The Narragansett fish bit freely,
the New World let no paupers starve.
Each summer morning in a skiff
I rowed upstream to loot haddock
and bass. And each winter night
in the white woods in a sleigh
I clawed over a young woman
till she said yes in the blankets.

There I spent, stark and looking,
as many lives as I had earned.
The big oaks thrived on sperm and salt,
later I'd know about whaling.
For then, the white night, the woman
so far from you I'd fondle dead . . . .

"No Parks bitch marries a Potter!"
roared my father over a grouse.
Isabella Parks her name:
later she loved a boat-builder.
Good for him, though I had her first.

Enough. My mother washed my shirts
of her and wept until I ran.
One Sunday while the pious met
I bundled my goods and hid them
in the pines behind my father's house.
Nine that night I slipped out "to bed,"
and hid in the woods till the flush
of day. Then I walked west for luck,
and someday, when wealthy, for love.

In Hartford in a month I earned
six honest dollars, then faced north,
thought the chill in my breast deserved
an equal chill in the ether.

Lingering ghost, my wife, I'd be bent
three times over for you not
to please, to provide! Those wasted years----
how many chairs I caned for you.
At eighteen I could've been rich
if I'd stuck to one trade awhile.

See, I wander . . . .
             These skull-eyes I've
spent on tired gods hold cities----
one million Londons to Hell
and back. I skipped you, a tombstone,

downtown to catch one last dawn
more than we've bled together . . . .
This is vanity, vanity
is the fool to cinch my saddle . . . .

I felt those young breasts breathe me in;
I felt the frontier dark touch me
with a mother's bloody hands,
felt the sigh of the underworld
love me as if I wore its flesh.
Part of the earth then, as pebbles
and mice, still I could lose myself
as a fish-hawk loses itself
against the sun but still must dote
on fodder of the world below.

But I must be clever: I stand
with all that English dirt gone stale
and piled around me in chunks,
and nine children doomed and rigid.
after years of vermin and pox.
I'm a letter to myself
home in America; it please
Congress and God. No soul of mine
but's wasted on a stranger's flag----
here I feel the moonglow reflame
all the foxfire secrets of woods
and Indians and beaver.

My two years in New Hampshire----
to remember them feels as good
as a backrub, now that I'm old.
I'd cut a thousand acres
in my mind if I could relax,
now that I'm nasty and tottering.
Anything to talk myself
seaward and home---- yes, I'm home
as I'll get, and graveward: so what?
I'd give my true religion
a word to plant, let the tree bloom,

dark angel-fruit be its prize.
I want none, or a pension. . . .
Choosy I am: the wounds bicker
still for a bit of reward.
I'll come to that.

                    I took a barge
north to Lebanon, pay four dollars,
I had to sue to collect.

The river nights were one sweet flush
of iron down the evening hills.
On watch till dawn, poling upstream,
I dreaded beast and stars: each glint
of nightsky a fragment of breast
beneath the blanket. Then the teeth----
great dreams of teeth, as if I knew
what hunger would stalk me later
at the edge of the slum, the edge
of the mind where sea serpents play.

So much for my faith when I sued
first the bargeman for my wages,
then worked four months for acreage
the owner never paid me.
Cheated, I shot and trapped to buy
a hundred acres; cleared thirty,
I should have stayed.
                    All these barrens
of verse---- like my cleared acreage,
I ask, "What about the rest?"
It's all there, like bears in a cave:
some dark body in a dark place
where no one stalks without a gun,
or a god with a good stout stick.

Here I drift, headless. No gods there
but God, the rest were Mohawks,
but scared me almost as much
as a mob of Olympians.

No mercy suckled the trees, but
arrows and bear claws manured
more than a few with carcasses.
Listen: these were my good works:
I cleared by summer; trapped and shot
when the snow filled all the spaces
between the upheaved stones. I swept
on snowshoes through the thick woods
with a grace I could have dreamt
I'd learn only through a further life.

When I'd farmed for two years plus
I sold my acres, complete with bears.
Home to Mother, she swept me up
as if she'd found my bones glowing
one lovely night in bed at last,
and could hardly wait for the feast.
My fiance had given up.
Her family's house stood empty,
the front door swung in the breeze
with a cry as if of kittens.
No oil lamps glowed within to mime
the bright dreams she used to string
beadlike around her pale, bare neck.

She once had loved me, but the glaze
on her flesh was of obedience,
my fault was her obedience,
I'd wanted her to punish me.
On hot green days in August
when the light wind lifted skirts,
I gazed into mossy places
and wept. I had to strap my hand
to my thigh to keep from sinning.

So, dear wife, I signed on a ship
full of lime and hoops and staves.
We thought we'd make Grenada,
but after fifteen days of sun
and a healthy wind all the way

we took water into the lime
and the fire sunk us---- that quick.

Rowing, we met a Holland ship.
I made it to Eustatia, joined
a whaler for sixteen months.
There I learned to kill on order----
flailed blubber till both hands shook,
learned to lust for the poor whale's grease.
Back to Nantucket steeped in oil;
then I slooped to Cranston and back,
then three years of whaling in the Azores----
and so I practiced growing old.

Next I took north to Coventry
to farm the kindly summers by,
to forget how her breath had matched
the breath of corn and willows
as they strained with heavy soil to mate
barrenly, yet glad for the breeze.

Somewhere I forgot that young girl
forever, except in writing,
dear skeleton, and began to turn
to you like a sunflower
to the sun, just before autumn.

Coventry days went long and lean.
I'd shot in New Hampshire so joined
the militia to keep my aim.
Murder was in the air---- murder,
but let's pretend it first was taxes
because the British made it so.
I knew little of politics,
but I'd let no king on my land,
nor those lobster bullies of his.

Concord and Lexington blew past,
leaving the countryside trembling.
One Sunday in April I slaved
double-time to leave a field plowed
before I marched to my bullet.
General Putnam had left a field
unplowed, they say, but so what?
I've heard it was his own field:
no contract demands you do well
by yourself---- only by others.

So the damned stepped forth to Charlestown.
We were brave sinners, all of us.
To make sure, I strapped a cutlass,
rusty but sharp, to my left thigh.
Down to my roots the fear bellowed,
as if seed had awoken
again, as if my hand had swept
the webs from between her thighs at last.
And whom should she love but my ghost?

All day toward Charlestown we wept
along, what we called songs and jokes
were ancestral terrors weeping
as many would a month later
among our breastworks. That hot day,
hot for April, everything blue
seemed flesh, and so vulnerable;
and everything green seemed old meat
and beyond all harm . . . .

                    In Charlestown
we lounged until June, the redcoats
corked in Boston while we camped.
I took to drinking rum. Why not?
You would have, all your passion spent
on gazing over distant cannon.
So the mind, spent on God,
flashes its candles for a sign,
and like Mr. Revere finds
its lights strung high where they belong.
Let me die now, dripping wax.
Let me lie here, all sores and crust,
don't ask why what was once brave
is now bones itself, like me.
On June Seventeenth, Seventeen
Seventy-Five, I lopped off some
poor bastard's arm with that cutlass.
I don't know how many I shot.

God bore me to England that in
penance both my arms should grow limp,
I should bury nine kids, a wife----
my unutterable old grayness
a flag, someone's flag thrust from Hell. . . .

The battle: a thousand of us
on Breed's Hill just after dawn.
It seemed a sunny enough day
through the cracks in the cannon-smoke,
through blossoms of the firebombed town.
Our redoubts protected our shins
only, while we faced a shelling
pointblank from Copp's Hill Graveyard.
Colonel Prescott kept us digging.
My coat flapped as the shells spun past.
I was glad to shed it with blood.

I shot pretty fair on the Hill----
I would've earned my deerskin
that day, if redcoats were deer.

After three tries they overran us:
we poor preachers well-versed in "rights"
were short on powder and bayonets.
Cut off though we seemed, a few men
from Connecticut diverted
the flood; and so downhill we fled.
Not too far would we retreat:
to Cambridge; its burial ground
most welcome for the moment,
I thought---- hip-shot, ankle busted.

The surgeon knifed the hip clean,
the ankle took five weeks to patch.
Sacred now, that place: Bunker Hill
they call it, though we fought on Breed's:
Bunker Hill lay at our backs.
If we hadn't shot all our powder
we'd've kept the damn hill, slaughtered more
than the two hundred twenty-six
British we nailed. Still, we paid more
with one death: our Doctor Warren.
Now there's talk of a monument.
They should build it to match my slouch;
they could call the place "Potter's Field."
Oh, I've a little humor left,
not much. The ankle still pains me
now and then, but that's all right,
if Congress could pay me something
before I fold like a table.

Later in London a few drunks
claimed Yankees were cowards to run
at Bunker Hill. How many gross
of British need kill one Yankee?
I shut them up when I got old.
The damned roared and died right there,
it was good for me to see them,
good and cruel as a glimpse of Hell.
Don't forget I got mine in lead----
no glory, neither cash nor flag.

Dry as a monument, that day
still thickens in me as I speak.
We quartered on Prospect Hill.
There on the Third of July
General Washington took over,
and we howled as if fresh meat
had tempted wolves. For some odd lust
we'd live or die with him, we swore,
and like it.
                    Only gunpowder
stopped us then from taking Boston.
Who'd've thought we'd fight six full years,
then two more to peace? So virgins
go mad with victory at marriage,
then spend twenty years in battle
before the cruel old man will die.
What could I then spend on life,
calculating one more bullet
would render my thin hide worthless?
Former seaman, three years whaling,
I took to the brigantine
Washington, ten guns, to cut off
the British from seaborne supplies.

Listen, love: these nights in Boston
I can hear fresh headstones stagger past
as they try to find the sea. Meanwhile
we lie on the surgeon's table
while medical students grin.
So I dream we're restless with death
together, and wander from the plot.
I feel God drop plumblines to sound
me all the way through the belly
where gods aren't supposed to care, in
the groin where nine dead children stir.

Three days out of Cambridge we caught
a man o'war, the *Foy*. In trade
she caught us, eighty guns to ten.
So I was treated as a prize.
As I passed from ship to ship
December's gray Atlantic stirred:
that beast whose billion open mouths
would receive me if I willed.
Dear wife, forgive this thought: I wish
I'd leapt from the *Foy* that day
and drank all the ocean I could.

In Boston Bay the frigate
Tartar shipped our crew for England.
A sad, limp bunch we were, forty
sullen enough to dote on blood.
Right off we plotted mutiny;
but a renegade betrayed us.
As leader, I went to the brig,
where after a week in irons
I'd half-become iron myself.
So went the voyage: in Portsmouth
a month later we landed.

Because a British deserter
had betrayed me I was released:
no one will trust a traitor.
I was released to a hospital

where half of us enjoyed smallpox
and died with the neat map of death
in fine print on ravaged faces.
We who lived staged to Spithead,
where we languished on a guard ship.

After a month of cabin fever,
they let me row the officers
with a crew of British bargemen.
We took a lieutenant to shore
where the crew found an ale-house.
There, excused for nature's call,
I sped to the trees.
                  Ran four miles,
walked six more. Then an officer
called from a public house, "Ahoy,
what ship?"
              Foolishly I said, "None,"
and kept my pace.
                  A deserter,
he thought, half-right, so chased me.
"Stop thief!" he yelled. Houses emptied,
and after a mile they caught me,
panting. Stranger to the land,
I told the truth. The officer
dragged me to the inn with soldiers.

There he went upstairs with a whore,
while the two soldiers, seeing me
a real Yankee, ordered me drink.
God, we drank! The villagers
drank with us, made mock of me,
made me dance---- a "real Yankee dance"----
so I sweated and sobered up
while the soldiers went slowly blind.
The good and faithful of King George
kept the liquor poured and foamy,
glad to glimpse a demon rebel.
They thought me less than a Briton----
their version of the caveman----

more savage than even a Celt,
anxious as a pirate to kill.
I thought of that severed arm,
still the snake of my nightmares.
Could've belonged to the brother
of any of those drinkers.
But I could hardly doubt our war
when I heard those fat red peasants
droll their stupid insults on me----
slaves to their tiny island minds.
So I kept them talking all night,
until closing when the landlord
slumped vilely drunk behind his bar.
No anger had I spent on fools:
my Yankee jig had amused them
while it kept me sober enough.
They thought me fair enough at dance,
and said so as they tipped the bowl.
Good enough for me: my keepers
began to swim in slipping eyes.
What a dream that night seems now----
as far as a planet and gone . . . .
I've never had the cash to drink
since then a whole evening through.
Sad. Rum's good grease for stiff old meat.

Again I escaped: up a wall
and over, while two drunks stroked
the shadows to feel me hiding.
First I tripped them both, though handcuffed;
too dark of mind and night to search,
they fumbled on the wrong side
of the garden wall, fumble still,
dead in Eden, for all I know.
Bellowed like bullocks for awhile,
then probably fell in stupor.
So I set out for fifty years
or so of stupor of my own.

Dear one, you were the only light
in fifty years of London mist
after my few years as a spy
and gardener, lacky to a king
I couldn't help respecting.
Still in my British Sailor's suit
at dawn, I met a scarecrow
and offered to trade him my clothes.
Princely though my pants he squinted:
"Runaway," he muttered,
                              then, "come,"
and something about his "church suit."

He dropped his tools by a hedge
and took me home to his squalor.
Never in America such
a misery, no stable
but has its horse-blanket, no bed
so much less than a manger.
                              Five kids
he kept here, much as a poor black
on a poor Southern farm, I'd suppose.
If I'd known I'd make him look rich
by comparison with myself
before my exile had expired,
why, I'd have turned myself in
and spent the war on the guard-ship
instead of risking my neck
for rich and soft Mr. Franklin
and the Congress that keeps me poor.
The old scarecrow liked the trade,
though one leg of my trousers
would have served his whole thin body.
So I stepped forth in fresh rags----
felt like wash in the waiting.
No turkey'd ever been more plucked,
but well I broke myself in.

I asked the way to London.
"Lunnun? I dunno, fifty miles sound right?"

Miles they were, but more like eighty,
at least, I learned through my shoes.
"Country's fulla soldiers lookin
for the odd-pence for deserters."
But he wouldn't betray me----
he wasn't crazy for soldiers.

I burned up thirty miles that day,
and spent the night in a barn
without so much as a single straw
to soften my half-captive dreams.
Half-captive still: for what fed
the dream but the freedom tainted
by deaths I'd taken for my own?
That night on a half-cured sheepskin
I felt the dark crawl on dog-feet
and try to lick me clean of hope
and love, to leave me as polished
as an old soupbone in the grass.

I dreamt stranger things, too: black bears
that wore gloves, like good gentlemen,
but carried nooses and seemed sad;
hunters dead and glowing in the grass
where branded wives mumbled by campfires
while I stood near, dressed in ashes.
And when the moon set, I felt one
long tooth bury into my neck
to drink from underground streams.

Dawn found me stiff as I've remained:
the mock-Israel you met
and loved, though you never loved me.
Harsh? I'm sorry, I loved you well,
but I must have been a statue,
a waxwork statue of a Yankee
molded for the sport of fools----
and for thirty-seven years
you loved a statue best you could.

Toward dawn I entered a large town.
A thousand slate-gray windows sharp
for deserters and reward.
Whittling a crutch, I played cripple,
and all the town avoided me,
fearing I'd beg for a pence,
or at least expect some pity.

Sadly, I met a real cripple.
"White swelling," I said when asked.

"Just my ailment, but you look worse,"
replied the other.
                    I stumped off
quickly, my face a great red bloom.
A good wagoner picked me up,
but after a mile I found him slow,
so leapt down, tossed my crutch, and ran.

No more big towns for me, I swore:
too many windows with faces,
too many ransacking soldiers.
I took to the open country:
still the villages were too close,
and the landscape full of ditches
and walls and hedges and streams.
One ditch, near twenty feet across,
believe it or not, I jumped dry!
One last night in some filthy barn,
and then, I thought, London.
                              But
not yet. In the small town of Staines
four British soldiers grabbed me,
saw the seaman's collar I wore,
thought me a runoff sailor.
So slam! into the Round House,
a flimsy jail, with no food----
for three days now I'd fasted.
Hunger drove me to violence:

I crushed my handcuffs on the wall,
sawed them across the window grate.
With their loosened bolt I picked
the padlock on my cell door
and ran. It was midnight. By dawn
I'd reached the village of Brintford.
I'd six pennies on the guard ship.
Now I was down to just four.

"Is there work hereabouts?" I asked
a man whitewashing a pale fence.
"Can you garden? John Millet hires
gardeners at this time of the year."
He explained how to find Sir John.

Off I strolled, up a gravelled walk:
good God, it led to the mansion
of the Princess Amelia!
Redcoats by the dozen!---- I ran
before they saw me, like a bear
at the sight of a firebrand.
The next path led to a gravel pit
where sweaty laborers shovelled.

"Help needed here?" I half-whined.

"Why, wait a bit, Master Sir John
hires a few about this time.
Wait here and he'll be along."

Too hungry not to chance capture,
I waited. Tyrannical,
purse-proud I'd heard the English Lords,
lackeys, boot-lickers for the Crown.
I wanted to hate Sir John
when he strolled up dressed to shame;
but he seemed kindly enough,
asked me whether I had a hoe,
then said he'd supply me one.

Then back to the village baker.
Now brave, I bought two tuppence loaves,
demolished them both in moments.
Then into a wrecked carriage-house
for the night. A ragged phaeton
served me as a cradle till dawn.

Possibly it was the small wink
of kindness that persuaded me
Sir John would become my patron:
perhaps my half-starved brain fed on
visions it sucked from the ether
to comfort it for lack of food.
But that morning I felt sure
my future would surpass a dog's.

With a huge iron fork and hoe
I began to transport gravel,
though with such obvious weakness
my fellow workers felt pity.
Poverty hadn't brutalized them
as it surely does so many.
Sir John watched me struggle, then asked
did I feign, why was I so limp?

"Ain't eaten for a week," one
new friend embellished my state.
Sir John, amazed, pressed a shilling
into my hand for meat and bread.
My belly thanked him in growls
which would have flattered any bear.

That night Sir John ordered a bed
in the barn, where I slept on straw----
that night the best sleep of my life.
The next day Sir John bid me spend
the morning abed. At dinner
he came to see me, and asked,
"So you're a seaman. Tell me how
you came here. I won't betray you."
Sure he wouldn't lie to me,
I told him everything I could,
from when I joined the militia
till I foundered on his kindness.

"You Americans have your friends
here in England," he assured me.
"You'll be safe in my employ.
All the soldiers, though, are bandits.
They constantly prowl the country
for deserters. For a few pence
they'd betray their closest friends."

We talked a little of the war,
though he wouldn't call it a war,
he called it an "eruption."
"England can't win so far from home.

A waste of good tax money,
of lives and supplies and good will,"
he claimed, and I guess he knew right.

I had doubts, though, I'm sorry to say.
"We were brave enough on Breed's Hill,"
I told him, "but powder ran short.
England can cut us off by sea."
"Your Doctor Franklin works on that,"
Sir John replied. "He's got some plan
he's trying to push with the French."
I didn't know what that would mean
to me a few months later.

Blessed with a new suit from Sir John,
I made a six-months' contract
to hoe his strawberry garden.
That term over, I went to work
for the Princess Amelia,
thanks to a good word from Sir John.
There the talk was of "damned rebels,
coward Yankees." I held my tongue
for awhile.
            Finally I heard
a vile word about Rhode Island
militiamen and how they fought,
and something about our mothers----
so I flattened the man who spoke.

Fired and lucky to keep clear of jail,
I hired out to a farmer
in a small suburb of Brintford.
Three weeks later rumor claimed
me as a Yankee on the loose,
and the redcoats were after me!

I don't know how anyone knew----
maybe the fight that got me fired.
They searched hard for me, driven
by greed: if it weren't for some friends,
who seemed friends of my country
as well, they would have snared me.

Once I hid in a garret
when the soldiers came to search.
I leapt from bed, seized my clothes,
and through the scuttle reached the roof.
Half-naked I crossed a dozen
roofs as if they were stepping-stones.

So harassed from place to place,
finally I found a berth
with none less than His Majesty,
old George himself, as gardener
on an estate of his near Quew.
There I felt safe: no soldiers
would dare disturb the royal premises.
No one then suspected me
an American escapee, but
before I'd been there a week
even the king heard the rumor.

That summer the king himself had come
to walk away his war worries.
Often I saw him in his gloom,
long-faced among the arbors.
I could have killed him if I'd pleased----
but he looked too human, too sad
and too much one with the quiet
gardens droopy in vines and buds----
a bit of antique statuary
all mossy as if with longing
for the vegetable world around.

One day while I gravelled a walk
His Majesty accosted me:
"Of what country were you born?"
he asked, as grim as some old stump.
"American born, may it please
Your Majesty." No way would I
hide my heritage in shame
from my country's worst enemy.

He answered, "Put on your hat, then,
you rebels foreswore allegiance."

He laughed and said, "Oh you're stubborn,
all of you. So why are you here?
A long way to travel for work."

"War's fate." This was melodrama!
"I was a prisoner awhile."

"And now?" Already he seemed bored,
as if he knew all this already.

"I escaped. I fought on Breed's Hill----"

"Breed's Hill? You bastards flogged my soldiers!"
But he was laughing again.

"Yes." I dropped the Your Majesty----
he didn't seem to notice.
"Now your soldiers harass me,
though I'm helpless enough now,
and no danger to anyone."

"Well, why not join my army then?
Safer with them than against them.
Yes, join then." He looked worried,
as if I should pull a pistol.

Looking down, I shook my head.
He could never understand us.

"You're stubborn, you rebels, stubborn.
Yes, stubborn. Well, you're safe enough
in my gardens. Gravel the walk,
then, gravel away."
                          Still growling,
this tame lion stalked off to haunt
the garden further, thinking gray thoughts.
No longer, if I ever had,
could I dream of murdering him:
he now seemed too real a man,
more a man than any redcoat
with a bayonet and musket
to do his talking for him.

I continued as His Majesty's
gardener for nearly four months.
Then with autumn I was discharged.
I raked hay on a private farm
for awhile; the rumors caught me,
and again I was on the dodge.
Such worry---- I almost gave up.

One day a certain luck befell.
I had known we Americans
had our friends here in England,
possibly even His Majesty
himself, despite the bad advice
of ministers and Parliament.
(I was wrong, I much later found:
the king's benign face had fooled me.)

One night while I slept in the barn
my farm-boss came with a lantern.
"Squire Woodcock's sent for you----
go see him tomorrow evening.
I'm pretty sure it'll be safe."

At first I thought this the soldiers'
crude decoy to entrap me.
But my farm-boss was my friend:
he'd never gladly give me up.
Squire Woodcock, besides, was suspect
in the neighborhood---- a Yankee
at heart, or so it was said.

So that next evening I went.
At eight I stood on Squire's porch
and glanced around.
                        "You're safe here,"
the Squire, a rumpled, blunt man swore.

Inside I found two other men,
gentlemen to judge by looks,
sipping expensive brandy.

"Mr. Potter, Mr. Horne Tooke,
Mr. James Bridges. We three
are friendly toward America
and want to help settle a peace.
If you're the hard-core Yankee we've
heard you are, we've a job for you."

A job? I thought they meant farming.
"No, you want to help your fellows,
though you're trapped here in Britain?
Would you care to travel a bit?"

"Explain," I asked.
                    "Not yet," he said.
"First tell us about yourself----
how you got here, what you want to do."

I told them I wished for no more
than passage to America.
Then I described my life, the fight
on Breed's Hill, my captivity.

Listen, my darling, if you can:
these men all are dead now. You may
meet their souls some airy day
in Heaven; be gentle with them,
they were friends to your Israel.

They found I loved my country still;
as if dreary England could win
affections hard-earned by New Hampshire
and its vast, dreamy forests;
as if a gray little garden
could tempt me to forget Rhode Island
and the fishing in Narragansett,
and my parents and childhood friends . . . .

I'd already gambled my hide
for my chosen landscape; no task
to wager it once again.
"But you talk like traitors to me."

"It's the British Constitution
we defend with 'disloyalty,' "
Squire Woodcock explained. "We insist
on our rights as you on yours.
'Country' is more than government,
freedom isn't a gift of the crown
but something we've earned for ourselves.
I couldn't betray one handful
of this beloved soil, but turn
on those bastards in Parliament?
Gladly---- first they'd enslave you
in America, then us
at home---- all, they'll claim, for the 'crown,'
but all in truth for their pockets."
I murmured assent, felt relief.
No one can trust a traitor,
but these men weren't traitors, no,
but rebels of a sort, as we.

"Would you take a trip to Paris?"
Mr. Bridges began. "We need----
we have---- or will have---- a message.
To Doctor Franklin. Important,
of course, or we wouldn't ask you."

"Of course we'll pay all expenses,"
butted in Mr. Tooke. "A bit
of compensation besides."

"And perhaps get you home besides,"
smiled Squire Woodcock, and convinced me,
though I would've done it anyway.
They offered me a guinea.

"Remove yourself to White Waltham.
We'll send for you there. Be sure
to come as soon as we call.
Here's a letter for Mr. Cray
of that town. Hold out your right foot."
"Why? Do I need new boots?"

                                        "Oh yes,
indeed yes," laughed the Squire. "New boots
for Potter, yes you'll have new boots."
After a glass of good cognac
I took the road to White Waltham.

Mr. Cray seemed glad to meet me.
He had war news aplenty,
and was anxious to dispense it.
"You know you Americans
have gone for secession," he laughed,
a happy, brick-orange man with ale
on his breath and on his waistcoat.

"So no more chance of compromise?
What about all the loyalists?"

"Hell no." He was a vicar.
"Tories and loyalists be damned,
they're all a bunch of bloody sots.
Your congress declared itself
a defacto government,
and everyone's free except slaves----
no more kowtowing to the Crown."
He was delighted! Poor King George.
(What am I saying?---- Stop me!)
I was pleased to hear the Congress
had chosen the long, hard way.
Free of English greed for cotton
I thought we could free the black slaves;
free of English taxes we could
free ourselves from unpaid labor,
earn what we needed and no more.
We could deal with the Indians
man to man, without redcoats
prowling the woods to panic them----
I thought there seemed plenty of land;
all that acreage in New Hampshire
and New York, and so few settlers . . . .

I was wrong. I couldn't see
how what I thought was English greed
was ours as well, and would strengthen
after we severed from England----
we'd still be human, too small
for the landscape we'd learn to fear.

Ten days later a note from Squire:
"On the stroke of two A.M.,"
it warned me. A good Gothic plot.

In an iron rain, I arrived,
my cheap shoes crumbled from my feet.
"Good thing we made these boots for you!"
Squire Woodcock laughed. "And look----"
the left heel pivoted: he poked
a letter into the cavity.
"Make sure Doctor Franklin reads this.
Now try these on, walk a little----
that's it. O Jesus, they creak!"

"That's alright," said Horne Tooke. "He looks
the sort of man whose new boots would creak."

With money and directions
I strolled to Charing Cross to catch
the post-coach to Dover, then
a fast packet to Calais.
Fifteen minutes after docking
I was on the stage to Paris.

The French were friendly enough.
They saw I was American
right off---- sharper than the English
who, after so many wars
and a new one brewing, they hated.

Not speaking the language, though,
I had trouble with the streets.
Finally I found a sooty house,
big enough but sort of shabby,
as if all it needed was a bath.

An old man cobbling shoes called
in English, "What do you want?"
I wondered if he'd made the boots
I wore. He'd recognize them
if he had, but he showed no sign.

"Doctor Franklin, " I answered,
and he seemed pleased with the reply,
as if he'd just won a bet.
Upstairs I was left to knock.

"Enter," and there stood the Doctor
in a rich gold dressing-gown
embroidered with roses and winged
monsters with many human heads
and algebraic and holy
figures mingled together.
Everywhere in the room lay books
and papers and scrolls and toy
machines and strange instruments,
like an alchemist's playroom.
On the wall barometers hung,
and maps and diagrams and cloth
geometric tapestries.
The walls themselves were gray and cracked,
as was the Doctor; but both
seemed to bloom with Franklin's soul.

Or so I imagined---- those years
of fame and philosophy had honed
him as a fine old dinner-knife,
consecrated by ancient meals.
He was seventy-two then,
and his back was turned to me.

"How do you do, Doctor?"
                                    "Aha,
I smell maize: an American.
What's the news? Something special?"
Squatting, I yanked off a boot.

"Too tight, eh? Well, that's fashion.
God should've given us iron
to shoe instead of flesh---- and would've,
had he seen how---- oh, wait!"
He dashed to the door, slammed the bolt,
drew the curtain across the windows.
"So we must interpret those boots,
I see," he said as I detached
the heel and pulled out the message.

"No vanity after all,"
he mused, "but a sort of prudence.
Now let me look at those papers."

For half an hour I sat
while he read and reread what I'd brought.
He looked up, newly curious:
"Now tell me about yourself.
I read here you're an escaped
prisoner of war, and trusted.
Tell me more."
                    I told him all,
and how I desired passage
home as my only reward.

"Well, I think I can procure that."

I must have looked too happy,
for he added, "But maybe not.
These are difficult times, you know."

I felt as though a plum-pudding
had appeared under my nose,
then gone rotten before I bit.

"Spend a few days in Paris
and I'll send you back with papers.
You'll have to make a return trip,
and then I'll try to ship you home.
There's a room waiting for you----
you'll have to be my prisoner.
No sightseeing, I'm afraid:
I'll need you on such short notice.
Business before pleasure; and now
a bit of pleasure. Will you lunch
with me in my rooms? It's best,
being poor, you avoid cafes.
Why dine out when you can dine in?"
So he sent out to a restaurant:
we got lamb boiled with green peas,
and water to drink.
                    "Why no wine?"

Doctor Franklin looked impatient.
"Here you'll drink water. Wine? Why,
what per glass do you think wine costs?"

"Say, three English pennies, Doctor."

"For rotgut. And how much bread
will your three pennies buy?"
                            "Why, three loaves."
"And how many glasses might
a man drink at one meal?"
                            "The vicar
in White Waltham drank a bottle."

"Alright, thirteen glasses, then.
Figure it out yourself. The man
drank thirty-nine pennies. In bread,
why, that's an extravagance.
Why was he such a glutton?"

"Doctor Franklin, he drank wine by choice.
If he'd eaten thirty-nine loaves
of bread of course he'd be a glutton.
For wine, though, one bottle's nothing.
Bread? He hardly ever ate it."

"Didn't he? He drank the money,
therefore he drank the loaves. Money
and bread to all are the same."
He left it for me to puzzle.

After a few minutes he rose.
"Now leave me until this evening,
peruse this book, if you will."
It was *Poor Richard's Almanac*,
which I'd read a hundred times.
"And there's your room. Take comfort,
and soon you'll see home again,
though hope too hard for nothing."
Hoped to hard I must have, though.

After two days I packed by boots
with fresh new letters from Franklin
and left Paris for Brintford.
No trouble. At Squire Woodcock's
I rested a few days, then staged
once again for Paris. This trip
would be my last as courier:
after returning to Brintford
I'd turn around again for France
and Doctor Franklin would ship me,
he said, for America.

But no such luck for Israel.
Just three hours before Dover
to ship the last time for Calais,
war broke between France and England
and all intercourse was cut off.

So God saw me fit for exile:
first of my race doomed to wander
because of some unscriptured sin.
I suppose every new nation
has to loose a few outcasts
like maple seeds winged on the wind.

War's the price: we're all killers.
Every nation's founded in blood,
self-pity, self-righteousness . . . .
A few of us, like that poor Jew,
will always have to prowl the earth
on aching feet, thirsty for the balm
that might make all men gardeners again.

But we were right!---- damn it, why
apologize? I'm not sorry
either to God or to men that
I shot a few redcoats: only
that I didn't shoot a few more!

Suffering's made me pompous----
Doctor Franklin would be amused.

Benjamain Franklin,
Né à Boston en 1706, mort le 17 avril 1790.

No hope of sailing to France
(the Channel too wide to swim)
I turned back to Brintford to mourn.

Squire Woodcock consulted his friends.
"I can't stay here, I'm too suspect,"
I told Mr. Tooke. "No dungeon
for me, I think London's safer."

They agreed. In laborer's clothes
and with a pocket full of coins
I left. Those good men gave me
five guineas for Americans
confined in a City prison----
where I'd go too, if not careful.

That evening I took lodgings: five
shillings weekly in Lombard Street.
There I was a Lincolnshire man----
they'd know I'd no London accent.
The next day I found the prison:
black as a man o'war, grimmer
than the Cambridge cemetery
where the Breed's Hill dead lie buried.
Only by bribing the turnkey
could I enter. On the threshold
a prisoner surprised me
by yelling "Potter---- is that you?
How in the Hell did you get here?"

The turnkey went rigid at my back.
It was an old friend named Singles
who had shouted. With a wink
I warned him to keep his tongue.
"Who do you think I am, mister?
I'm just a Lincolnshire farmer,
never been to London before.
My master owed a trifle
to a rebel trader who asked
the balance to go to fellow Yanks

he'd heard were imprisoned here.''
The turnkey shook his head and left.

Fifteen Americans kept here
in a cell of eighteen foot square----
furnished with a ten-foot bench,
a heap of straw, some horse-blankets
the horses had died from under.
There seemed nothing I could do.
I pitied them awhile, then left.

I spent five days exploring,
then took a berth as a coachman
for J. Hyslop, rigid but fair,
at fifteen shillings weekly.
Staying sober, I quickly saved
a pretty good amount of cash----
more in six months than in the whole
first twelve I'd spent in England.

But luck failed once more: I was fired.
Wandering for work on the fringe
of London one gray afternoon
I came across a huge brickyard.
There I'd work for five muddy years:
for brickmaking's playing in mud----
six shillings weekly plus all
the mud I could or cared to eat.

I worked in a mixing mill:
a hopper and a tub where dough
for bricks was mixed by horsepower
while men poured in clay and sand.
I was a moulder---- ladled dough
fresh from the mill into trays
which were the molds for the bricks.

For five years I ladled dough,
and ate more than my peck of dirt.

No promotion for me, a Yank.
In the summer I gardened
as well, for the sake of good green air.
The brickworks convinced me God
and men were doomed to go gray
and ragged, like thunderstorms.
That's why He made us in His likeness
and of clay with a touch of salt.

One of the London poor, I lived with thieves
who'd murder for the odd pence
here and there; beggars, swindlers,
pickpockets, pimps and footpads
haunted the dismal evening streets.
One night in Hyde Park, five pounds
in a secret pocket, pennies
in my pants, six pistolmen
stopped me, searched, took the pennies.
In Bow Street Barracks
an officer told me that night
that gang had robbed eight people.
"Clever they are," he observed.
I doubt that gang was ever caught.

So I grew thin and cramped by labor.
That brickyard was the Dismal Swamp,
or Bunyan's Slough. Every day mist
and cold, or raw heat and sweat----
and yet London had to be built.
No shelter for us dumb beasts, though:
there on that barren moor the bricks
were spawned by the thousands daily,
and went to their various fates
without a murmur of complaint.
I suppose I became a brick
myself: and why not?

                    Remember,
my dear wife, when I met you?
I was brick-orange with the clay

and you laughed, but not too harshly.
My god, you seemed crystal by contrast:
polished I could see a future
in you; but I missed the death's-head.

Forgive me. When I married you
my fortunes fell, as if the ghostly
love I'd spent on that Rhode Island girl
secretly as cancer would haunt us.
So on I labored, married now,
new slave to British industry,
supporting with my withered bones
the nation I'd set out to fight.
We kept a room in Red Cross Street,
remember? And for a few years,
though in bondage close as the Jews'
in Egypt, still we were happy.

In October in '81
Cornwallis surrendered. All London
mourned as if a typhoon had swept
the city, or as if thunder
had announced in plain language
the death of all one's closest friends.
But in the brickyard no one cared.
"All's vanity plus clay,"
we liked to tell each other
as we slapped and spattered the dough.

Quietly I was pleased; and you,
you pleased me more with your pride
in my countrymen, pleased me
with this humble proof of your love.

Stalemated, the war festered awhile
till Lord North's majority failed.
In March of '82 he resigned.
The war had brought its excitement:
the coastal raids of John Paul Jones,
which made the British lion howl;

the soldiers in the streets, threat
of an invasion by the French.
The war had brought prosperity,
but it was fragile, too fragile . . . .

Meanwhile, babies had begun
to arrive: pride in fatherhood,
the death of most in infancy,
kept us breeding till you'd borne ten.

I shouldn't have forced them on you----
yet you were silent even
in the agonies of labor.
You never pushed me from your bed.
We were so poor, though, and the poor
make babies to keep themselves poor:
such is the pride God takes in us
that He gives the poor extra doses
of what makes men humble and wise
in fairy tales---- hardly in life,
where the poor resemble hung meat.

Forgive me that, but I wonder:
do the rich have one god, the poor
another? I once thought England
bore a cruel god indeed; but now
his shadow dims America,
dark as the lash on the backs
of black slaves.
                    Can we afford
a god so cruel? Have we founded
New Eden or a charnel-house?

I'm preaching again, my darling,
but old men are given to preach
because we think we've learned how
to heal all wounds but our own.

His Most Sacred Majesty GEORGE the III. King of Great Britain &c.

Printed for Carington Bowles, in St Pauls Church Yard.

Each day England endeared me less.
Surrounded by mugs and rogues
I wept every day for home.
City life in London's a dog's
life and death---- kicked from gutter
to sewer and back again.

Even some of the beggars
were rogues at the core: wealthy men
dressed to excite pity and pence.
Even now my bird-cage chest
swells with anger as I recall
the first day I had to beg:
it's still a stone in my gut
after these forty or more years.

I thought when the treaties were signed
we'd all ship to America.
But there wasn't passage for us
all, I the only citizen----
and how could I pay for the rest?

You said, "Leave us, send money
later when you're settled and rich."
I was two men for awhile,
then I choose you. I'm not sorry----
not even America breathed
or smiled as deep within me
as you did in your years of life.

So once again a woman mapped
my life: in revenge I mapped yours
with the scars of ten hard childbirths
I hadn't thought were punishment
until you punished me with death,
your own.

          You died on Guy Fawkes Day----
a misty day of gunpowder.
I would've leapt from London Bridge,

if not too weak to climb the rail.
You remember.
                    But long before,
in '83, the brickworks failed.
In the glut of former soldiers
work was scarce: so you suggested
I learn to cane chairs, and I did.

Now I've caned thousands of chairs.
Even in hospital when
my bones felt only fit for soup
I caned chairs to pay my way.
I hope in Heaven or Hell
or Purgatory no one sits
on cane chairs: for if they do I'm
doomed to recane all Eternity's
worn-out chairs.
                    Even God Himself
will bellow, "Who's the chair-caner here?"
and I'll raise a limp coward's hand,
then apply my art to the Throne.

We were lucky we didn't starve
sooner: London was full of thugs
who needed work and would get it
over an honest man, most jobs
no more honest than most men.

Little work without a war.
The brickyard had failed, and gardeners
more plentiful than sewer mice.
Even in chair-caning hundreds competed:
a dozen might fight for one chair.
Wages fell, street criers thronged
the streets with services and wares.
Among them I cried "Chairs to mend"
hour after hour in the dim streets
choked with starvelings and prostitutes.

The sickness that struck our children
year after year drained my wages
till I spent some months in prison,
a debtor. I would've died there
if you hadn't gone to the streets.
Oh, I knew. I couldn't complain,
too broken, and half a ghost . . . .
You sold your body to save me----
what was it but a bag of meat
hardly fit for the butcher?

My creditor was a dragon:
he snarled and wept when you paid----
he'd rather I had died for him.
I weighed eighty pounds when released.
Never since have I been well.
I had nothing to forgive you,
I was the breadwinner, and had failed.

Did I suffer? I never stole----
some poor friends were doomed to crime
and prison; the poor make clumsy
criminals.
             The law doesn't care if
a good man's children lie in mud.

So the famine crept through England,
making crooks or beggars of most.
We stood in luck awhile, then I
fell ill, our children died one
at a time, more wars came and went,
and we grew old and pale and bowed.

Napoleon made us money:
for a few years we had fresh meat,
there were plenty of chairs to mend.
What kind of life is caning chairs,
though, for a man who's hunted
and trapped in the northern forests,

heard eagles cry in fire-stripped pines
and the loon mock Adam's madness?

We buried seven infants
and two grown sons. Only one boy
I've now, spared by a bitter god
who likes to gobble up children.

Without the help of this last child
I'd still be sifting rags and glass,
or stiff in a London alley.
Now at least I'll die at home.

When Napoleon's war ended,
banditry and famine again
swept England, city and country
alike.

      I became a rag-picker
to supplement my chair-caning.
People died in the streets and lay
sometimes for days without notice.
My last son, seven years old,
went to work with me: he caned chairs
better than I, though so young.

I was seventy-three years old,
he should have been my grandson.

One day I took ill. For six weeks
I couldn't work or pay the rent.
Do you remember the cold day
our furniture was seized for debt?
We'd had nothing of value,
but then we had nothing at all.
So we lay on the floor. And first
I began to cry, then you,
and our child, quietly, at last . . . .

It was on that floor your stroke came,
on devil's feet while we slept.
You were paralyzed at dawn----
I don't think you knew me
from that moment until you died.

I had to beg a few pennies
to have you hauled to the hospital.
Then they wouldn't take you in because
you'd married an American.
"Let the Yankees support their poor,"
they said.
                    There were, though, kind men
I applied to, who paid your way.
One a vicar who thought kindness
was carrying out God's work.
I didn't want to argue,
but God's work is obvious,
and has no charity in it.

Too late for you we returned
with money to the hospital:
you lingered a few days, and died.

With the sole child of my old age
I moved to a furnished room.
Four shillings and sixpence a week.
Chair-caning, between us we just
made enough to cover the rent
and a little food, mostly fish.
The furnishings weren't much: one bunk
of straw, two chairs, a table,
and one iron kettle for cooking.

All day we'd both cry for chairs
to mend, and when there wasn't work
my son would sweep public causeways,
hoping for tips from gentlemen.

Grown infirm, sometimes I'd sit home
and make matches which we'd sell,
if lucky, in public markets.

One night returning home alone
in the rain, all my matches unsold,
a butcher took pity on me----
emaciated, dripping ragbag----
and threw a beef-heart and yelled
"Get home and cook that right away,
if you've got a home to get to."
That night the beef-heart saved my life:
I hadn't eaten for three days,
and the beef-heart eaten, wouldn't
eat again for another three.

Another day in Threadneedle Street
while I was crying for chairs
a gentleman stared at my shoes,
then handed me a new half-crown,
saying, "Go cry 'old shoes to mend!' "

Shame had entered and settled me,
I can repeat this without blushing.
Too old even to cry, I seemed

no longer home in my body
but following, like a shadow not
my own. I report this coolly,
I want nothing more than I've earned.

The long winter evenings I spent
telling my son about the house
in Cranston, and how I grew up
without knowing children caned chairs
to feed themselves in London.

A year after you died, dear wife,
I took ill and would have
joined you in the potter's field----
but I had to live for my son
a little longer.
                    Poor Thomas----
for three weeks he worked alone
for a few pennies a day.
He began to try to talk me
into trying to get a passage
free from the American Consul.

"You'd be left behind," I answered.

"I could save my money and sail
later." As if he earned so much
he could start a bank-account!

I promised to see the Consul,
though it meant a two-mile walk,
and I was so feeble it took
all day for me to make it there.

The Consul at first disbelieved
I'd been born an American:
that's how English I'd become,
though most Englishmen could spot me.

He questioned me carefully though,
and after my long account
believed. "Still, the government
won't pay the passage for your son----
and good God, you're so old and weak
you'd never survive the voyage."

"I won't go without my son."
I rose, tottery, to return.

Now my son began to cry.
The Consul stammered, "Wait awhile,"
and after considering, "Look,
I'll pay the child's passage---- half-fare
for his age. I have relatives
in Boston, He must stay with them,
you're too feeble to bring him up.
If that's alright, your son should go
on the London packet Tuesday.
You, on the other hand, must stay
abed awhile; fatten you up
for the voyage. I'll pay your board.
I'll charge it to expenses----
you're a citizen, it's alright."

After a moment's discussion----
some doubt about this charity,
some doubt about separation----
we agreed that if I lived
I'd join my son in Boston
in only a few weeks' time----
and if not, he'd be better off fed
in Boston than starved in London.

A hard few weeks, but stingy
with life I squeezed it out lengthwise
and spread it till it might fit.
I weighed ninety pounds on shipboard,
half again my weight before.

My ship was the *Carterian*----
London to New York in April
1823. Six weeks,
and spent with Americans,
or so some of the crew claimed themselves,
though they stole the clothes from my back
one comic night at knifepoint
so that I arrived in New York
at midnight wrapped in a blanket.

Home after close on fifty years . . . .!
The captain gave me clothes for shore.
At dawn, first off the ship, I took
passage for Boston right away.
There my son met me on the wharf.

Well-fed for a change, half grown,
he seemed, since I'd seen him last:
"I've had pies and puddings daily,"
he chanted. "I'm half sick of them."

That afternoon in Charlestown
I stood on Breed's Hill----fifty years
since I'd caught my two bullets there.
Only a pasture now, quiet
despite the houses in rows
close around it. So long I sat
in the grass my son grew nervous,
as if I'd turned to salt upon
this landscape of outmoded deaths.

No surprise if I had; nor if
I'd woken suddenly sure
I'd died on that battlefield
and since had dreamt in the grave
of an exile further than death.

A week later in Roxbury
I took leave of my son and hiked

to Cranston to see what pittance
might remain of my father's farm.

When I got there strangers, lawyers,
told me not a cent, no rod of land----
all gobbled up by my brothers,
who've long since pushed their way west
and most likely have long since died.

I was never paid for service
in the Continental Army----
not that I'd served so very long,
unless my servitude in England
be counted, as some said it should.

Broke and with little future,
I petitioned Congress for the
pension other aged rebels,
what few are left, have received.

Together with the deposition
of a respectable friend,
Mr. John Vials, my petition
went to Congress with all my hopes----
and yet for no other reason
than my absence from the country
when the pension law was passed,
my petition was rejected.

LIFE

AND

REMARKABLE ADVENTURES

OF

ISRAEL R. POTTER,

(A NATIVE OF CRANSTON, RHODE-ISLAND.)

WHO WAS A SOLDIER IN THE

AMERICAN REVOLUTION,

And took a distinguished part in the Battle of Bunker
Hill (in which he received three wounds.) after
which he was taken Prisoner by the British, convey-
ed to England, where for 30 years he obtained a
livelihood for himself and family, by crying " *Old
Chairs to Mend*" through the Streets of London.—
In May last, by the assistance of the American Con
sul, he succeeded (in the 79th year of his age) in
obtaining a passage to his native country, after an
absence of 48 years.

PROVIDENCE:
Printed by HENRY TRUMBULL—1824.
(Price 28 Cents.)

No reflection had ransacked my sleep
since that night spent on a sheepskin
fifty years ago. No sorrow's touched
me the way this wrinkled new world
has touched me, naked in my old age.

I'm shocked because we still keep slaves,
I might as well be slave myself.
No altruist: just facts of cash.
We're still enslaved to the dollar,
our taxes are still a complaint.

I'd thought we loved our liberty
well enough that it would love us
back, and calm all that cruelty,
spread a salve on all whom it touched . . . .

So what's the point of this pity
I've wasted on a pensionless man
when we could pity the world?

Was it just a lie we took to bed
when the stick-fire faded to ash
and we cuddled our own dry ghosts?
We conceived a country in war.
So they all come about: nasty,
but no more than man and woman
in begetting their children----
a little nakedness and blood.

It's what we do best: kill and eat,
and make babies to mimic us.

Dear wife, you grew up outside me,
I met you as trees meet in groves.
But this country is in my dream
the way a seed's in the bole.
It can't survive without me
to go on dreaming how I killed
maybe a dozen men for it;

it can't see itself but in me,
as if I'd polished all this grief
to hold up to a great, shy face
and beg---- beg for what? Not money,
I'll never have that, nor love.
Maybe for the nine children
I spilled with my clumsy hands,
for the one child left to me here . . . .
And that shy face---- no one sees it,
but it's watching, it seems sorry
it's not a god, has no power
to so much as bathe; and this life,
the greed, and we still keep slaves!

You, my dear wife, you watch me too,
and now and then drop with a star
to stroke my face, swimming through the cool
autumn nights: breath upon steeple
and common and bone-white homes.

Peace to you: you're rid of the flesh.
Spirit, bless these smug villagers,
bless even the slaveholders,
pity all the farmers who'd cheat
their best friends for a hog. And bless
this groaning engine as it flails
feebly a few more strokes, then fails.

Pray that the gods forgive small debts,
that late on some frost-riddled night
an aged bear, desperate for love,
will spite the human landscape: he'll
claw out a passage to share
my cubby beneath next winter's snow.

Then landscape'll mate with dumb force:
now the passion and ghost shall rhyme,
and beast and brain will hit zero and
so dam my fable's reckless source.

NOTES

Page

9   "Dear wife." Potter at the age of eighty prepares to dictate his autobiography to Henry Trumbull. Potter imagines his dead wife is with him.

11   "the moonlight reflame/ all the foxfire secrets." Some people believed that foxfire absorbed moonlight to regurgitate on dark nights.

14   "I took north to Coventry." In Rhode Island, about 62 miles southwest of Boston. Potter's militia company could hardly have marched to Cambridge in one day, as he later implies.

16   "on Breed's Hill just after dawn." The actual battle began at three in the afternoon. The Committee of Safety had, on June 15, resolved "unanimously that it be recommended to the Council of War that . . . Bunker Hill be maintained by a sufficient force being posted there . . . ." Breed's Hill, where the battle was actually fought, was actually a minor summit of Bunker Hill, closer to the harbor and Boston than the main summit. Whether the original intent was to fortify the main summit of Bunker Hill, whether Prescott became lost in the dark, as some historians suggest, whether he deliberately chose on his own to fortify Breed's Hill, is uncertain. Apparently General Putnam had no complaint about Prescott's choice of territory, so perhaps Breed's Hill was the intended location all along.

17   "they could call the place 'Potter's Field.'" Matthew 27, v.7: "So after conferring they used it to buy the Potter's Field, as a burial place for foreigners." *New English Bible.*

18   "I took to the brigantine/ *Washington*." The *Washington*'s history is short and slightly unsavory. She was launched on August 23, 1775, built by John Wharton. Her first captain was Henry Dougherty. Sion Martindale took over later, and was in command when the ship was captured by the British frigate *Fowley* off Cape Ann in December, 1775. William Watson, on November 29, 1775, wrote to General Washington "that the people on board the brigantine *Washington* are in general discontented and have agreed to do no duty on board said vessel, and say that they enlisted to serve in the army and not as marines . . . . His people really appear to me to be a set of the most unprincipled abandoned fellows I ever saw." Later, however, the success of the *Harrison* seems to have cheered the whole navy. On December 4 Watson wrote, "After repairing on board the brig Saturday night, inquiring into the cause of the uneasiness among the people and finding it principally owing to their want of clothing, and after supplying them with what they wanted, the whole crew, to a man, gave three cheers and declared their readiness to go to sea the next morning." Quoted in *A Naval History of the American Revolution* by Gardner W. Allen.

23   "more like eighty." Spithead, off Portsmouth, is 83 miles from London by the route Potter probably took.

24   "a large town." Probably Aldershot.

    "'White swelling.'" "A form of swelling without redness. 1803: *Medical Journal*, IX, 374." (O.E.D.)

25   "the village of Brintford." Correctly spelled Brentford.

    "the mansion/ of the Princess Amelia." The Princess Amelia was a daughter of George II, and therefore an aunt of George III.

29   "an estate of his near Quew." Kew Gardens, Kew Palace, and the Queen's Cottage: "built about 1772, a favorite garden house of King George and Queen Charlotte." Ogden, *London for Everyone.*

29-30 The conversation with King George is partially taken from Melville's *Israel Potter*, as is the conversation with Franklin on pp. 27-30.

32 "Mr. Horne Tooke." (1736-1812) "The son of a poulterer named Horne, who added the name of his friend William Tooke to his own in 1782." *Oxford Companion to English Literature* p. 825. Tooke certainly lived in Brentford in 1778, but Potter could hardly have known him other than as John Horne. Perhaps Henry Trumbull emended the later, more famous name. Tooke was a founding member of the Constitutional Society, which on June 7, 1775 "passed a resolution which was published in the newspapers. It directed that a subscription be raised on behalf of 'our beloved American fellow subjects' who had 'preferred death to slavery,' and 'were for that reason only inhumanly murdered by the king's troops' at the Lexington skirmish. Horne was to pay the money to Franklin." Horne spent a year in prison for his part in this affair. *DNB* Vol. XIX, 967-974. Melville, in *Israel Potter*, notes that Tooke is the "famous author of *The Diversions of Purley* . . . then in the first honest ardor of his political career."

38 "He was seventy-two." Franklin was born in 1706.

41 "war broke." The Anglo-French War began on June 17, 1778.

43 "a City prison." Probably the original (and notorious) Newgate Prison, burned in 1780 by the Gordon Rioters.

"in Lombard Street." Between Cheapside and Fenchurch in the City.

46 "a room in Red Cross Street." Between Golden Lane and Fore Street in Finsbury.

49 "when the treaties were signed." The final treaty was signed on September 3, 1783, but not ratified by the congress until January, 1784.

"You died on Guy Fawkes Day." Potter is jumping over forty years. His wife died on November 5, 1821.

51 "Napoleon made us money." England was more or less at war with France from 1793 to 1814, but Potter probably refers to the period 1803-1814. Oddly, Potter never mentions the War of 1812.

53 "you'd married an American." Apparently no one took Potter for a "Lincolnshire farmer" anymore.

56 "joined you in the potter's field." Potter's pun is still deliberate but no longer self-amusing.

"I promised to see the Consul." Potter would have been further discouraged by a comment on his plight written by a later American Consul, Nathaniel Hawthorne, in the 1850's: "It was my ultimate conclusion . . . that American ingenuity may be pretty safely left to itself, and that, one way or another, a Yankee vagabond is certain to turn up at his own threshold, if he has any, with or without help of a consul, and perhaps be taught a lesson of foresight that may profit him hereafter.

"Among these stray Americans, I met with no other case so remarkable as that of an old man, who was in the habit of visiting me once in a few months, and soberly affirmed that he had been wandering about England more than a quarter of a century . . . . and all the while doing his utmost to get home again. Herman Melville, in his excellent novel or biography of 'Israel Potter' has an idea somewhat similar to this." *Our Old Home*. 1884 ed. 26-27.

"The Consul at first disbelieved/ I'd been born an American." Hawthorne later expresses a similar doubt about the above "old man."

57 " 'I have relatives.' " The Consul's quick decision on such a complex and imposing situation amazes me, but Potter expresses no surprise.

58   "and hiked/ to Cranston." Remarkably, a fifty-mile hike. A few months before, remember, Potter had needed all day to walk two miles to the Consulate.
59   The pension issue is confusing. The Continental Congress in 1783 voted the officers of the Continental Army half-pay for life, the enlisted men full pay for five years at the conclusion of the war. Later, lifetime pensions were granted for all persons disabled in the war. Apparently there was still a later pension bill for aged veterans. Potter may simply have expected back pay, plus his five years' severance pay.

"Mr. John Vials." This deposition is reprinted in full in the first edition of *The Life and Remarkable Adventures of Israel Potter*. Vials repeats Potter's error in attributing the capture of the *Washington* to the *Foy* instead of the *Fowley*.

Books from Seven Woods Press

Susan Fromberg Schaeffer, *The Witch and the Weather Report*

Nathan Whiting, *Transitions*

Albert Goldbarth, *Opticks*

William Doreski, *The Testament of Israel Potter*